Little Mans Big Day

Lonnie Lesane Sr.

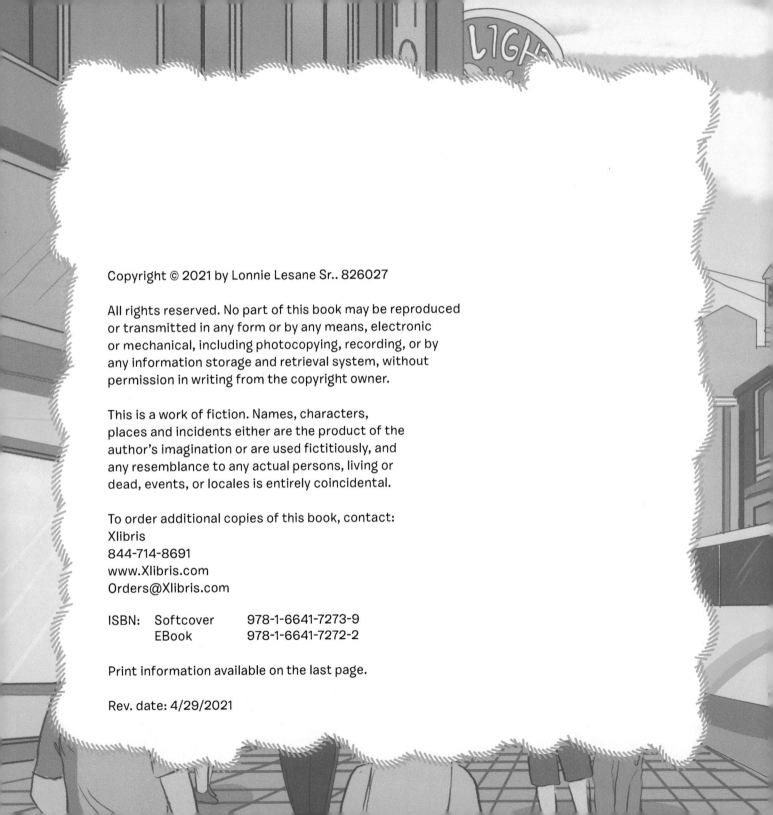

To order additional copies of this book, contact:
Xlibris
844-714-8691
www.Xlibris.com
Orders@Xlibris.com

ISBN: Softcover   978-1-6641-7273-9
        EBook   978-1-6641-7272-2

Print information available on the last page.

Rev. date: 4/29/2021

Little Mans Big Day

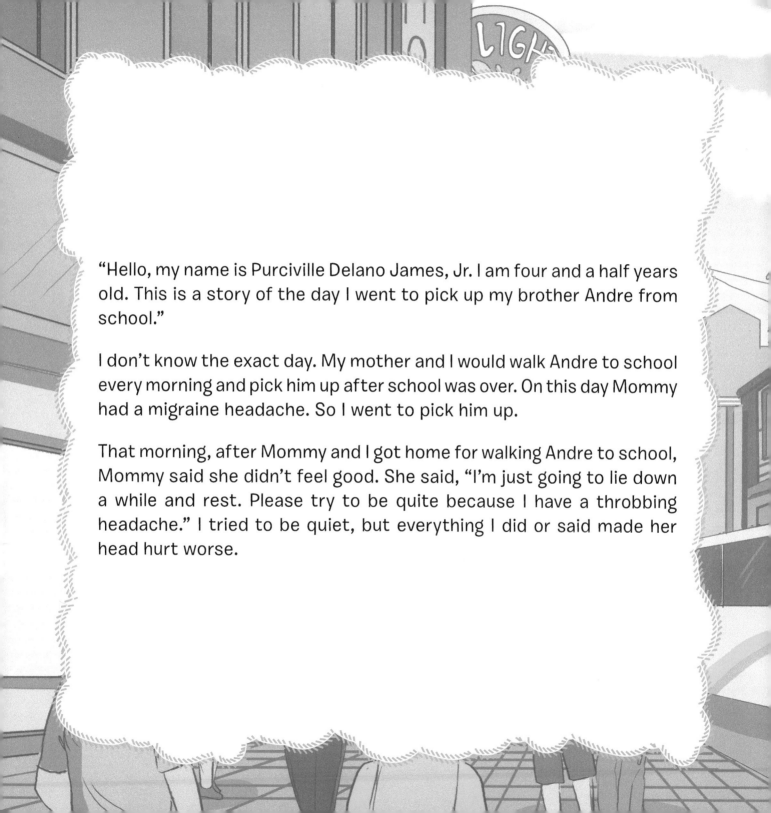

"Hello, my name is Purciville Delano James, Jr. I am four and a half years old. This is a story of the day I went to pick up my brother Andre from school."

I don't know the exact day. My mother and I would walk Andre to school every morning and pick him up after school was over. On this day Mommy had a migraine headache. So I went to pick him up.

That morning, after Mommy and I got home for walking Andre to school, Mommy said she didn't feel good. She said, "I'm just going to lie down a while and rest. Please try to be quite because I have a throbbing headache." I tried to be quiet, but everything I did or said made her head hurt worse.

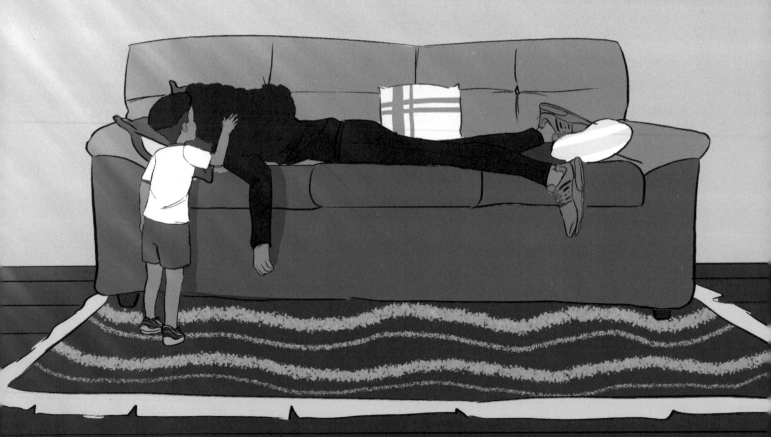

When she finally got to sleep, it was almost time to pick up Andre. I know because Batman was on. ''Mommy, Mommy,'' I yelled. "Mommy, wake up. It' s time to go get Andre." Come on Mommy, Batman's on, it's time to go get Andre."

Mommy said "Okay Percy," "That's what she called me.

Everybody else call me little Percy." But it didn' t sound like she was talking to me, but to somebody else who was probably in her dreams cause she said it as she was turning her head and bury her face into the couch.

So I put my shoes on, fetched D.O.G, put his leash on, and away we went out the back door, through the gate, and down the alley. You may have guessed, D.O. G. is my dog.

Now it only took me and Mommy ten or twenty minutes to get to the school. It really depends on whether we go through the alley or the longer way around Venessa Street.

"Ah man, the alley never looked this long when I was with Mommy." "Maybe I should say a prayer like Mommy." "Jesus, hole my hand please. Amen." "Come on D.O.G."

''Ruff,'' said D.O.G as he wagged his tail and hung out his tongue. With D.O.G. by my side and the prayer being said, we started walking towards the end of the alley.

Every sound in the alley was bigger than before. From the time we stepped into the alley, every sound seemed to be coming to get me. The rustling of the rats in the trash sounded like flesh eating monsters. It was like I was hearing them for the first time.

I can't tum back now. Andre wouldn't. He wasn't scared of nothing.

The usual growling and snarling coming from the backyards next to the alley seemed a hundred times louder than normal. My heart was beating harder, and my eyes got wider and wider with each sound. I could see those gigantuous monsters grabbing out for me. The barking dogs were grizzly bears, and the snarling cats were verocious lions.

The shadows lurking in the broad day-light were closing in on my. I looked over at D.O.G., and he looked fearless. But the lump in my throat was the size of a softball, so I held onto D.O.G.'s leash as tight as I could that I could not feel my fingers. The closer we got to the end of the alley, the louder the sounds got, and my heart was about to jump right out of my chest. When we finally got to the last house, which was empty, D.O.G. began to bark and growl at something. As fast as my little feet could carry me, I ran what seemed like a mile out of the alley.

Then O' begeebee! The cars were so big and were moving so fast I thought of turning back into the alley, but one look behind me and I quickly changed my mind.

I looked at D.O.G. who was looking at me as if to say 'Come on, let's go." He didn't know I didn't know which way to go. I could see the Green's store a few blocks away, and it was then I remembered Mommy sometimes stopped there to get candy for me and Andre. That's the way I'm going. D.O.G. was already pulling me in that direction as if he knew the way.

Now there was still one obstacle, we needed to cross the street. As we walked towards the corner a big bus drove past so fast that I felt I was caught up in a tornado. "Whew!" It was about a hundred miles long. It pulled the back of my shirt so tight until it felt like it would tear. D.O.G. seemed to be floating in the air like kite. It was scary, but it was also fun. People on the bus were pointing and shouting. Homs were honking and cars were passing and everything was aimed at me. Big cars, little cars, in between cars, all kinds of horns were telling me not to step in the street. They didn't know I needed to get Andre. I started a slow jog towards the Green's store.

As I got closer, Mr. Willie stepped from the storefront with his broom. Mr. Willie owned the store. He was a nice man with gray hair and he always gave Mommy candy for Andre and me.

"Lil Percy, what are you doing here?" Where ' s your mother?" "She didn't feel well. She has a headache," I replied. "So I am going to get Andre." He rubbed the top of his head, andsaid "Be careful now Percy, you and D.O.G. Be very careful.

"Ruff, Ruff," barked D.O.G., waiting for a treat. Mr. Willie reached in his apron and came out with a treat for D.O.G. Then he reached behind my ear and came back with a bag of planters peanuts that appeared in his hand. "thank you Mr.Willie, " I said. He smiled again and said you two be careful."

When we got to the comer across from the school. A chill went through my body. It felt like ice. It's a four lane road. I don't know I can't cross the street by myself. A police car pulled beside me. "If I don't look at him. Maybe he won't notice me." I said to myself. So I stood very still trying to look invisible. Then the deepest voice I ever heard said "Hey little man, come here." I didn't move because I was invisible and he couldn't be talking to me. He said it again. "Hey little man, come here." I turned towards him with legs shaking like spaghetti. I stuck out my chest and said "I'm little Percy, not little man." He smiled as he stepped out of his black and white car like the giant stepping down from the beanstalk.

"Boy what are you doing out here by yourself" he asked. "I'm picking up my brother Andre. Me and D.O.G.

"Aren't you PJ's son, he asked. My father's name is Purciville Dalona James, Sr." I answered. He laughed again as if he knew me. And he reached down and picked me up in his arms and said again. I know your father. He and I we went to school together. Are you okay?" he asked.

"Get him D.O.G., get him. But D.O.G. looked up at me with his big puppy dog eyes and almost smiled a sinister grin. I guess he was scared of the beanstalk giant and not even a ferocious dog like D.O.G. can bring down a giant. As I looked at him, "ummm mmmmmmm, he moaned.

"Sure," I replied. Me and D.O.G. are going to wait here until my brother Andre gets out of school." "Okay" he said as he let me down. I'11 come around in a couple of minutes to check on you, okay."

"You mean you are not going to lock me up?" with both eyes wide open because I was afraid he was going to put me in the back seat of his car with the jail bars and haul me off in the jail on wheels.

He just laughed and returned to his car. I looked over at D.O.G. and said "some help you are." As we waited on the comer, seconds turned to minutes. Minutes turned to hours, Hours turned into days. Would school ever let out?

I heard bells, and I thought it was the school bell, except it wasn't. It just kept getting louder and louder and closer and closer. It got so loud, it was deafening. It must be an air raid. The enemy must be dropping bombs. This must be the warning.

I saw a big trash can behind me on the sidewalk, so before I knew it, I jumped into the trash can and pulled D.O.G. after me. Just as we dived in, an ambulance went past. The air raid was over.

Then another set of bells went off. "Oh no, not again" I screamed. I ducked my head back into the trash can. "The school must have gotten hit, maybe it is on fire. We have to save Andre, I said excitedly.

We tried to get out of the trash can, but it was not easy to climb out. But as we were finally able to get over the edge, we heard laughing and we were being pointed out. The kids were laughing as if a symphony of laughs performing like one of Mommy's favorite soap operas.

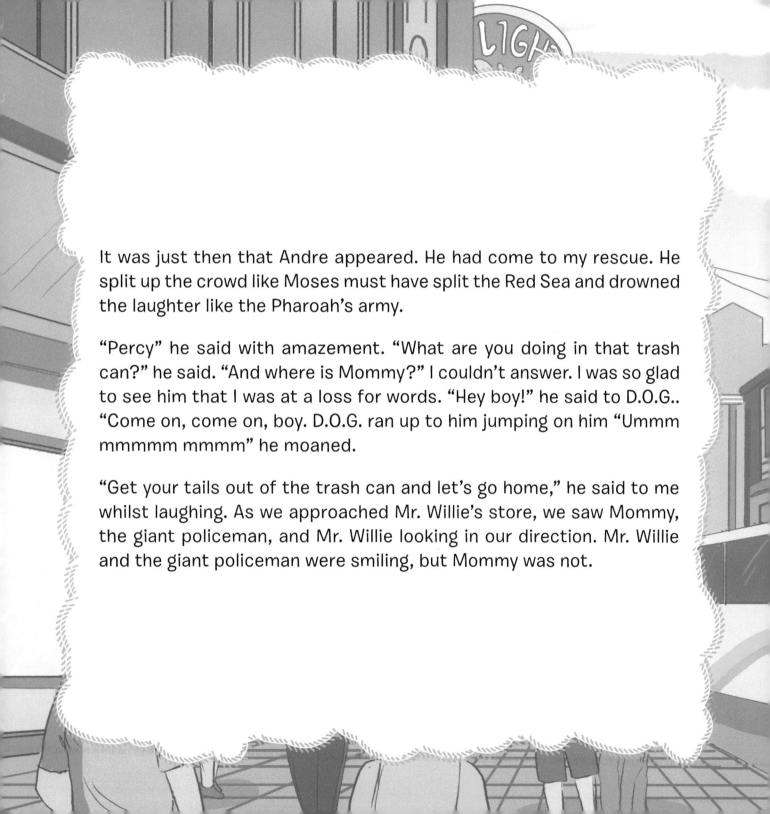

It was just then that Andre appeared. He had come to my rescue. He split up the crowd like Moses must have split the Red Sea and drowned the laughter like the Pharoah's army.

"Percy" he said with amazement. "What are you doing in that trash can?" he said. "And where is Mommy?" I couldn't answer. I was so glad to see him that I was at a loss for words. "Hey boy!" he said to D.O.G.. "Come on, come on, boy. D.O.G. ran up to him jumping on him "Ummm mmmmm mmmm" he moaned.

"Get your tails out of the trash can and let's go home," he said to me whilst laughing. As we approached Mr. Willie's store, we saw Mommy, the giant policeman, and Mr. Willie looking in our direction. Mr. Willie and the giant policeman were smiling, but Mommy was not.

CPSIA information can be obtained
at www.ICGtesting.com
Printed in the USA
BVHW021100280521
608374BV00009B/209